To Mom, who filled my childhood with
magic and made the best train cakes ever!
—Julia

To Trish, Kaylee, Liam, and Riley
—Ryan

Text Copyright © 2022 Julia Richardson
Illustration Copyright © 2022 Ryan O'Rourke
Design Copyright © 2022 Sleeping Bear Press

Sleeping Bear Press
2395 South Huron Parkway, Suite 200,
Ann Arbor, MI 48104
www.sleepingbearpress.com © Sleeping Bear Press
Printed and bound in the United States

10 9 8 7 6 5 4 3 2 1

Library of Congress Cataloging-in-Publication Data
Names: Richardson, Julia Marie, 1963- author. | O'Rourke, Ryan, illustrator.
Title: Let's build a little train / Julia Richardson ; illustrated by Ryan O'Rourke.
Other titles: Let us build a little train
Description: Ann Arbor, MI : Sleeping Bear Press, [2022] | Audience: Ages
4-8. | Summary: "From the boiler to the coupling, build a steam train
along with an engineer and her workers"-- Provided by publisher.
Identifiers: LCCN 2022006594 | ISBN 9781534111455 (hardcover)
Subjects: CYAC: Stories in rhyme. | Railroad trains--Fiction. | LCGFT:
Picture books. | Stories in rhyme.
Classification: LCC PZ8.3.R3965 Le 2022 | DDC [E]--dc23
LC record available at https://lccn.loc.gov/2022006594

Photo Credits:
Steam Train: page 28: The Everett Collection
Bogie: Photo 110919176 © Bulltus Casso | Dreamstime.com
Boiler: Photo 13955736 © Sinan Durdu | Dreamstime.com
Caboose: Photo 9752802 © Johnsroad7 | Dreamstime.com
Cattle Catcher: Photo 34285768 © Brackishnewzealand | Dreamstime.com
Coal: ID 151331822 © Evgeniy Parilov | Dreamstime.com
Coupling: Photo 73189333 / Steam Train Coupling © Junior Braz | Dreamstime.com
Piston: Photo 30514706 © Lovell35 | Dreamstime.com
Warehouse: Photo 42049436 © Arinahabich08 | Dreamstime.com
Weld: Photo 45309917 © Chorthip | Dreamstime.com

Let's Build A Little Train

JULIA RICHARDSON

ILLUSTRATED BY
RYAN O'ROURKE

PUBLISHED by SLEEPING BEAR PRESS™

Choooooooo!

Let's build a little train
to chug along the track
that goes from here to there
and circles round and back.

STEAM

PISTON

Sierra Railway No. 3

We'll need a giant warehouse
with lots of helping hands.
An engineer will manage
and supervise commands.

A worker cuts the metal to make the bogie base and welds it all together with goggles on his face.

A boiler goes above
with a box for burning coal;
six wheels of steel below
hook to pistons by a pole.

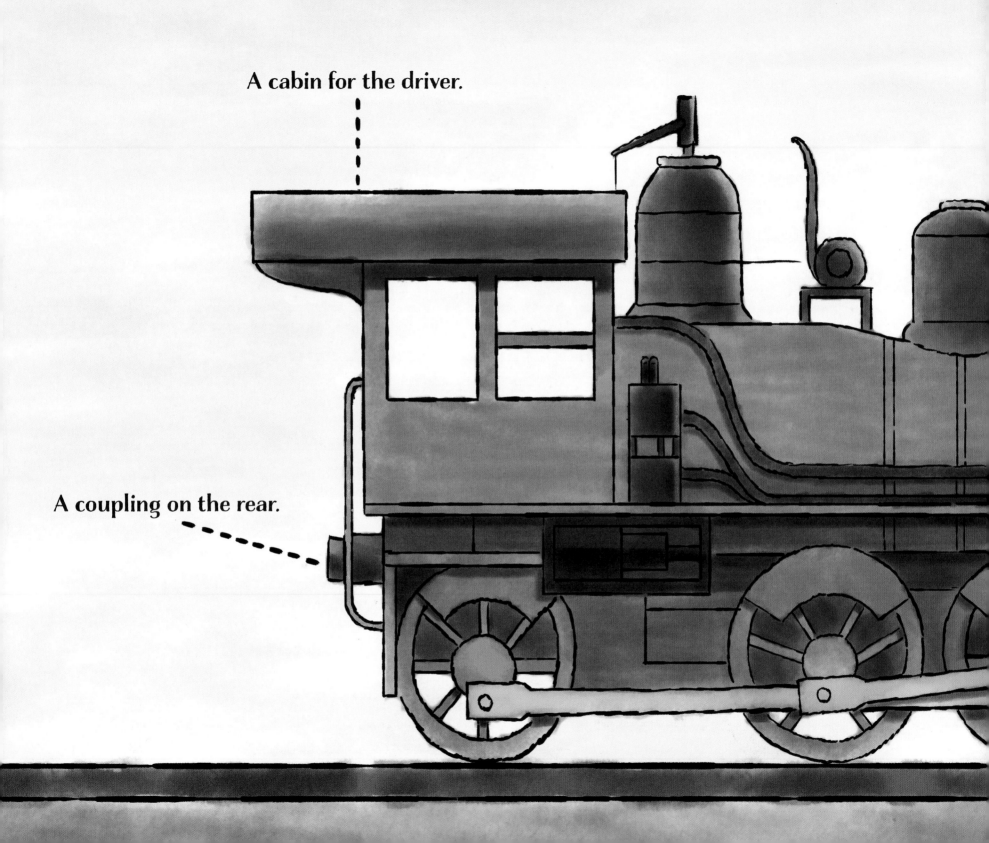

A cabin for the driver.

A coupling on the rear.

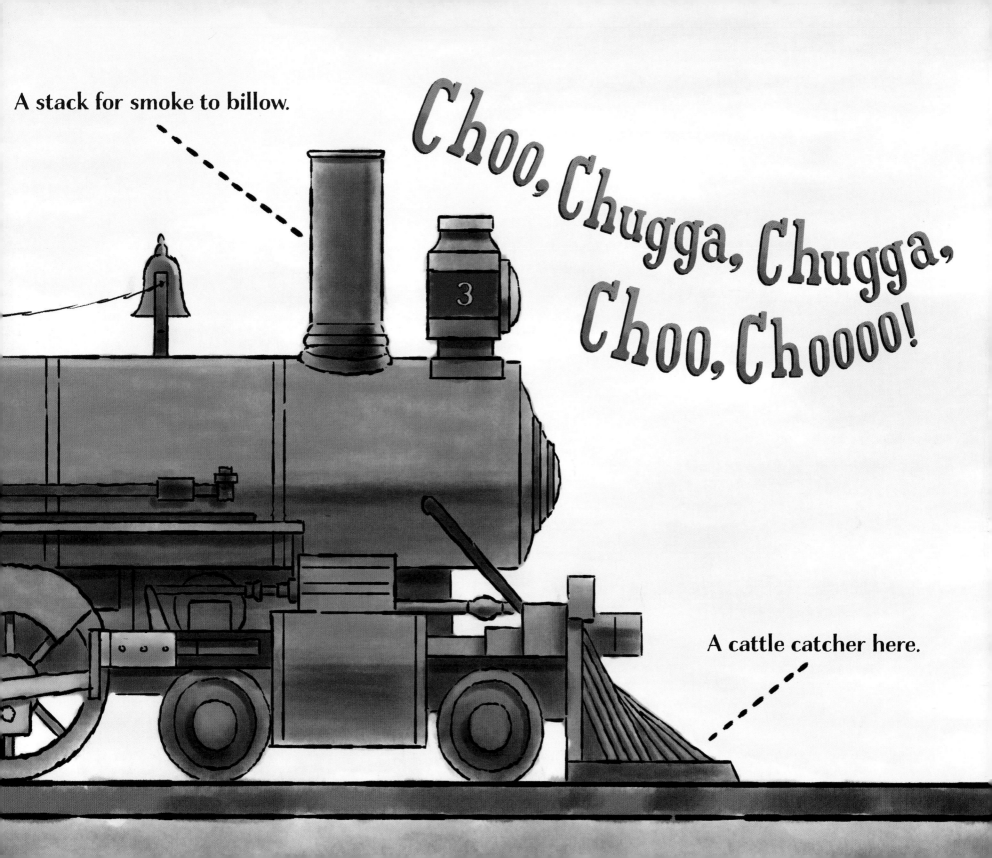

It's ready now for painting.
The colors make it glow.
All finished with the engine.
Let's see what it will tow.

FIRE EXTINGUISHER

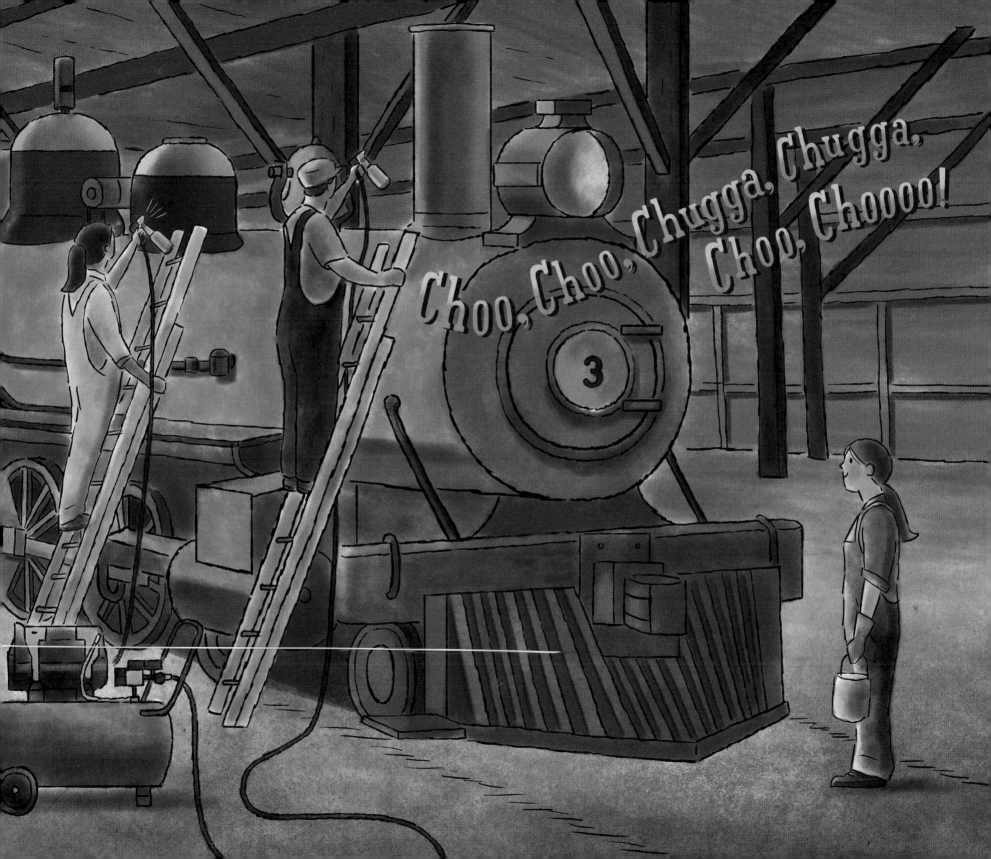

A cart for coal and water
to make the train go fast,
cars for hauling cargo,
a red caboose is last.

The driver climbs the ladder
and dons her cap of blue.
She hollers, "All aboard!"
and pulls the whistle, too.

Stoke the fire till it's hot,
boiling water in the pot.

Steam escapes, pressure grows,
pushing pistons. . . .

There it goes!

MORE ABOUT STEAM TRAINS

Before gasoline and electricity, trains were powered with steam. The steam was made by burning coal, which heated water in a large pot known as the boiler.

A tube that contained pistons captured the steam. As the steam accumulated in the tube, it pushed the pistons up and down.

STEAM →

WATER

COMBUSTION

COAL

PISTON

CRANKSHAFT

The pistons were attached to a pole that was attached to the wheels. The up-and-down motion of the pistons moved the pole, which in turn rotated the wheels and made the train move.

THE FIRST STEAM TRAIN was built in England in the early 1800s. It was heavy and chugged along at the slow speed of five miles per hour until it broke. With the invention of lighter and faster engines, railways spread all over the world. As steam trains replaced horses, people and goods moved between cities much quicker. This period of rapid change in history was called the Industrial Revolution.

BOGIE

The metal frame that supports the train and attaches to the wheels.

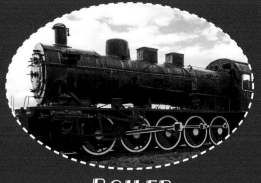

BOILER

The large tank that holds water in a steam engine.

CABOOSE

The car at the rear of a train where the crew eats and sleeps.

CATTLE CATCHER

A metal frame at the front of a train that clears the track of obstacles.

COAL

A black rock composed of ancient fossilized swamp plants that can be burned for fuel.

COUPLING

The device used to connect the cars in a train.

PISTON

A disc that moves up and down in a tube and makes an engine r

WAREHOUSE

s are made.

WELD

The process of joining metal together by heating.

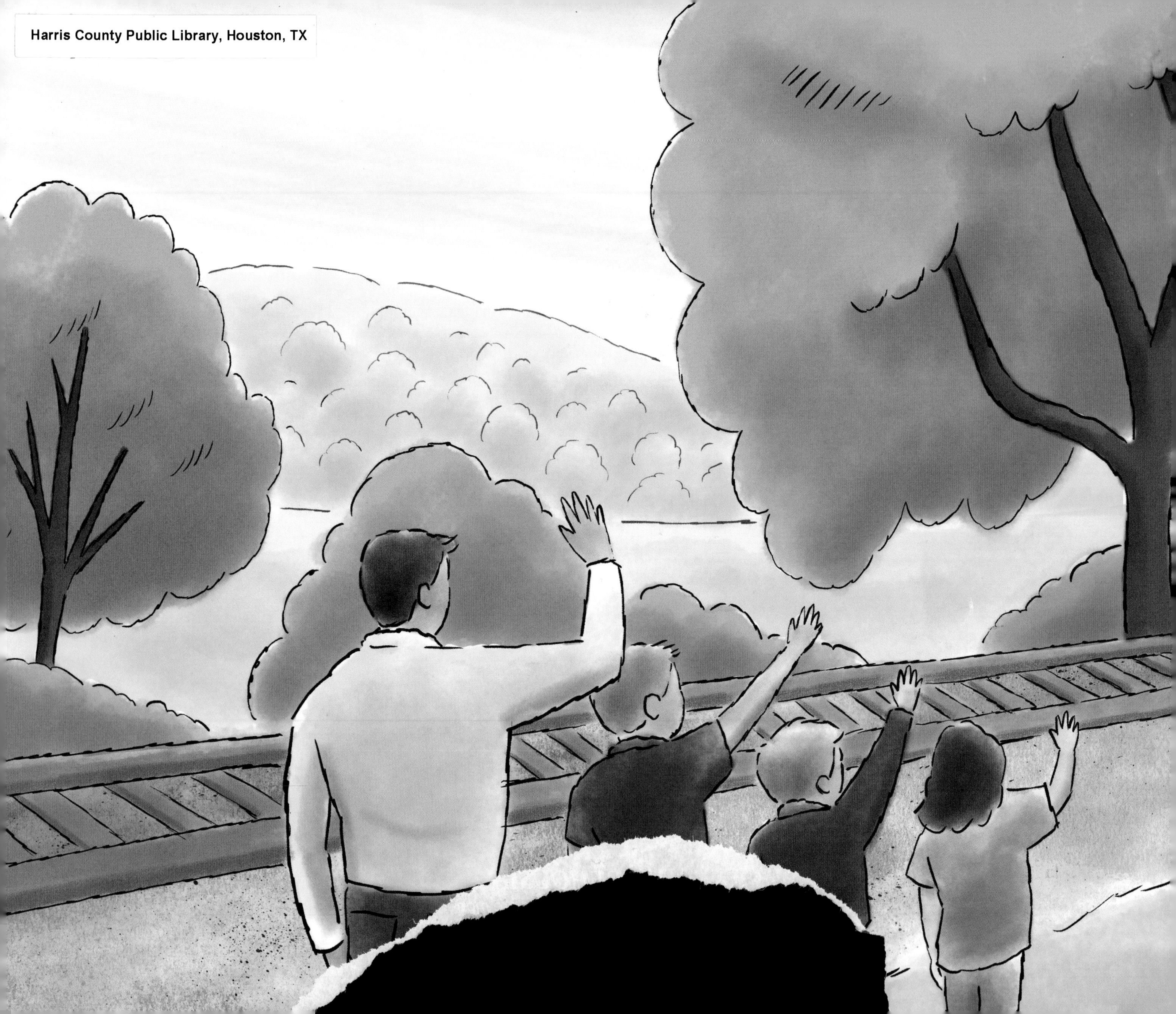

inspired
3D CHARACTER SETUP

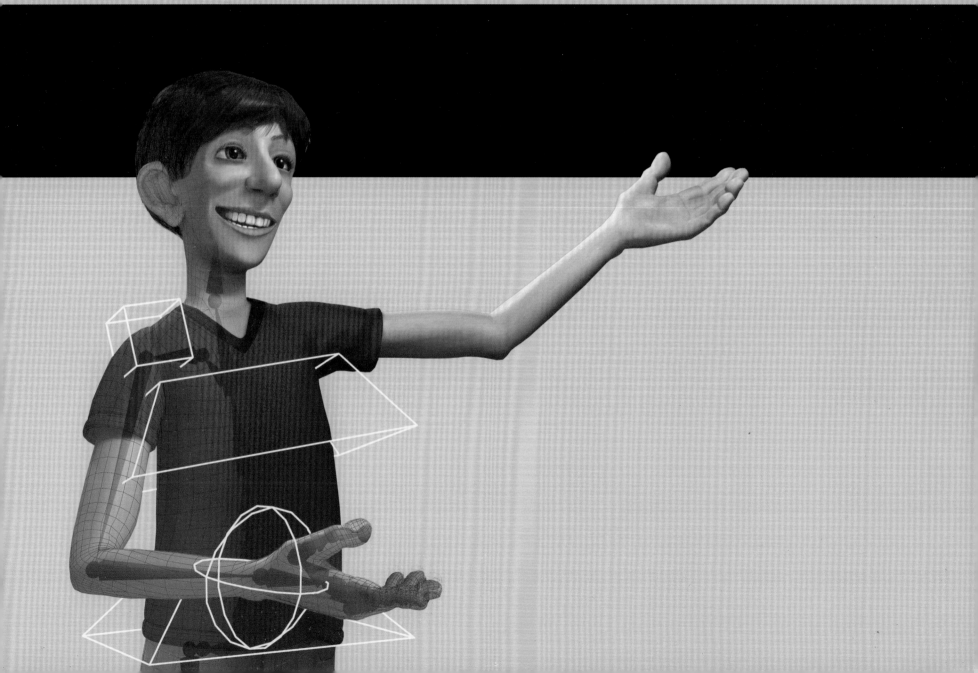